This book belongs to:

_____

Tushy Tanner

by
April Matula

little pink press™

Published by Little Pink Press, P.O. Box 847, Beacon, NY 12508

ISBN-13: 978-1-7329494-7-8

Tushy Tanner's real name was Timmy, but everyone called him Tushy because of his...er, eh...tushy! Yes, for a little olive-green frog, it was quite something. Tushy knew it was larger than most frogs his age, but around the house he really didn't mind.

Tushy could do lots of things such as carry his little sister around the house, pick up spills before his mom saw what he had done, and hide the pets he found in the backyard when his dad came home.

But when Tushy Tanner was not at home, having a large tushy was not fun at all. In fact, it was a nightmare!

At school, all the kids teased him. They would say, "Tushy needs a bench, not a chair," and, "Oh no, we're having beans for lunch...watch out for Tushy!"

Tushy felt very sad.

One day while Tushy was walking home from school, Creepy Craig called out, "Hey Tushy! What's it like carrying China on your back!?"

Tushy began to cry and hung his head so no one could see his tears.

As Tushy walked on, he saw a paper on the ground. "Litter bugs..." mumbled Tushy, and he bent over and picked it up. The paper read that volleyball try-outs were being held in the school gym at 3:30 that day.

"Wow," thought Tushy, "I really like volleyball! I'm going to give it a shot!"

When it was Tushy's turn to try out, he felt very nervous.
"Oh well, how bad can it be?" thought Tushy.

Then the balls came whirling his way...one, two, three,
four, five, six, seven, eight, nine, and ten! And, Tushy
was able to return all ten balls!

Coach Speedling was truly impressed. "Hey Tanner...you
made the team!"

Tushy felt so happy that he "ran-bounced" all the way home. He had to get ready for the first game tomorrow night.

Tushy practived his moves all night.

Finally he felt ready.

The next night arrived in a flash. Tushy felt nervous and excited as he joined his team on the court. He felt a little uncomfortable in his volleyball suit as the pants were a little snug. "Oh why do I have to have such a big tushy?" Tushy mumbled angrily.

Then he heard laughter, and someone from the other team called over to him and said "Glad you brought your pillow to rest your head on after we cream you! In fact, your whole team can rest their heads on that pillow!" Tushy felt embarrassed and hurt.

He wanted to go home, but he knew he was a team player and team players stick it out to the end.

When the game began, the ball seemed to gravitate toward Tushy. The ball was like a magnet, and he was like iron! "Yow!" cried Tushy, "This is great!"

He returned every ball, and thanks to his tushy, he gave the ball an extra spike! His team won 12 to nothing!!!!

The team gathered together and put Tushy up on their shoulders. "Hip, hip, hooray!" they yelled joyfully.

"Yeah Tushy!"

While Tushy was high in the air, he spotted Creepy Craig stealing Miss Fratz's purse.

"He's probably getting even for all those D's she gave him for Handwriting when he was in the third grade!" thought Tushy.

Without a second thought, Tushy jumped down and ran after Creepy Craig.

Run...bounce...tackle!

The next day when the school newspaper came out, it featured Tushy Tanner!!

"A little extra 'cushy' gives Tushy the edge!"

Tushy felt like a star!

Other books by April Matula:

It Happened Again

It's Going to Be Another Good Day

Lucky Larry

Oh, Lola!

Made in the USA
Columbia, SC
27 October 2020